W9-DGB-296

THIS WALKER BOOK BELONGS TO:

_____

_____

_____

_____

ROBIN HOOD AND LITTLE JOHN

One day, when walking in the forest, Robin
Hood encounters a huge stranger – and ends
up in the river! The man is John of Melton –
Little John – and he and Robin have in fact
met before, in a fight against Sir Guy of
Gisburn and his men. Now Little John sets
Robin and his men a challenge – to free the
lovely Clara from the clutches of the cruel
knight Ernald. The object is straightforward
enough, but the problem is not at all easy,
requiring cunning as well as courage – for
Clara is held prisoner in Conisbrough, whose
castle has the highest walls in the land. But
Marian suggests a way in which their arch
enemy Sir Guy himself might help!

WALKER STORYBOOKS

Staples for Amos by Alison Morgan
The Shape-Changer by Julian Atterton
Robin Hood and the Miller's Son
   by Julian Atterton
Robin Hood and Little John by Julian Atterton
Earthquake by Ruskin Bond
We Three Kings of Pepper Street Prime
   by Joan Smith

ROBIN HOOD
and *LITTLE JOHN*

First published 1987 by
Julia MacRae Books
This edition published 1989 by
Walker Books Ltd, 87 Vauxhall Walk,
London SE11 5HJ

Printed in Great Britain by
Richard Clay Ltd, Bungay, Suffolk

British Library Cataloguing in Publication Data
Atterton, Julian
Robin Hood and Little John.
I. Title   II. Dillow, John
823'.914[J]   PZ7
ISBN 0-7445-1395-2

ROBIN HOOD
and *LITTLE JOHN*

Written by
JULIAN ATTERTON

Illustrated by
JOHN DILLOW

WALKER BOOKS
LONDON

Contents

1 The Hooded Giant

In the heart of the forest of Barnsdale, the trees grew so thickly that their branches hung out over the highroad.

One summer morning, not long after daybreak, the branches of a great elm rustled then were still, as into them climbed a young man dressed in green. From his belt hung a sword and a hunting-horn, and from his perch he looked out over the forest the way a lord looks over his domain; and there was nothing strange in that, for this man was none other than the outlaw, Robin Hood.

Before long he heard a distant sound of singing, and he soon caught sight of two monks journeying south along the road, leading a

string of pack-mules whose baskets were
stuffed to the brim and covered with sacking.

Robin waited until they neared the elm, then
he set his horn to his lips and blew a peal that
sent a hundred birds flying from the trees in

alarm. The monks froze in their sandals, but before they had time to look up, Robin had swung down through the branches and dropped to the ground to face them.

"Greetings to you, my brothers," he said. "May I ask where you are bound?"

The monks were too busy rolling their eyes to reply, for at the call of Robin's horn, a dozen men had stepped out of the trees to surround the pack-train. Each was dressed in green, and they each carried a longbow of polished yew.

"Saints preserve us," said the elder monk. "Who are you and what do you want?"

"I am Robin Hood and these are my companions."

"Then we are as good as dead," sobbed the monk.

"Your thoughts are too dark for such a fair morning," said Robin. "I want your names, not your lives."

The monk took a deep breath and gathered his dignity.

"I am Brother Hubert," he replied, "and this is Brother Godfrey. We are white monks from the grange at Wentbridge, and we are taking our vegetables and cheeses to the brothers of Blyth Priory."

"Blyth Priory," exclaimed Robin. "I should have thought the monks there were rich enough to feed themselves."

"They would be, but for you," muttered young Brother Godfrey. He spoke under his breath, but not softly enough to pass unheard.

"And what do you mean by that?" Robin asked him.

The monk stared at his toes. "Blyth Priory has a guest-house for travellers on the high-road," he explained. "The brothers are always happy to shelter travellers for the night, but nowadays, whenever rich merchants hear that you and your robbers are in the neighbourhood, they hide in the priory until they think you have moved on. They are eating the monks out of house and home."

Robin roared with laughter. "Far be it from me to steal the supper of men whose purses I hope to empty," he said. "Good brothers, I grant you the freedom of the forest, and the right to pass without paying a toll."

"May the Mother of God reward you," said Brother Hubert.

"I thank you for your blessing," said Robin, "and I trust you will remember that you owe me a favour."

He was still laughing as the monks hurried on, but his good cheer vanished when he saw that his companions were glaring at him.

"Have you lost your wits?" asked Will Scarlet. "What do you mean by letting a rich catch like that slip through our fingers?"

"Oh, come now," said Robin, "you know yourself that white monks are rich only in land and what they make of it."

"Even so," said Much the Miller's son, "I would have given anything for one of their cheeses."

"Or some crunchy carrots," murmured Dickon.

"The bitter truth," said Will Scarlet, "is that every time we strike we put ourselves in danger. We cannot afford to play at being high-handed and noble."

11

Robin's eyes narrowed. "Listen to me, all of you," he said. "We swore when we became brothers of the forest that we would never rob good men, and that is how it will be for as long as I am your leader. Are you tired of your vows?"

The outlaws fell silent, but their faces were sullen.

"Well, I have had enough of lurking by the roadside for one day," said Robin. "I suggest we go our separate ways, and meet again this evening at the Camp of the Squirrels. Let us hope that by then our tempers are on the mend."

With that he strode into the forest, hardly caring which path he took just as long as it led him deep into the wild places, where he could be alone with his thoughts.

"A curse on all this," he whispered. "A curse on Guy of Gisburn for driving me to outlawry, and keeping me away from Marian my love, and a curse on the cruel times in which we live."

Robin walked until his anger was cooled by

the peace of the forest. Some hours later he was
dozing against a tree when the distant sound of
vesper bells told him it was time to turn back
towards the clearing where the outlaws had
their camp.

On his way homewards he came to a swift-
flowing stream over which a tree trunk had
been laid to serve as a bridge. As Robin stepped
onto it, a giant of a man appeared out of the

trees on the other bank, and without so much as a glance at Robin he stepped up onto the far end of the trunk.

"Not so fast, good fellow," cried Robin. "I was here before you, and I claim the right to cross first."

"Get out of my way, you dung-beetle," growled the giant, and he lumbered towards Robin so that they met in the middle of the bridge. Robin looked up at his opponent and shivered, for the giant wore a hood, and all that could be seen of his face in the evening shadows was a tangle of beard and a crooked row of teeth.

"It seems you need a lesson in courtesy," said Robin, and he thumped the giant in the chest. But the giant stood as solid as a rock, and before Robin could strike again he reached out with a huge hand and gave Robin a shove that sent him flying off the bridge into the stream.

Soaked and spluttering, Robin crawled up through the brambles and nettles of the river-bank to find the giant squatting on the ground, with his hands covering his face.

14

"That was not like me," said the giant. "Not like me at all."

Shaking his head sadly, he looked up at Robin, and after one good look at the giant's face, Robin gave a gasp of recognition.

"I know you," he exclaimed. "You came to my rescue in the market-place of Pontefract when I was fighting for my life against Guy of Gisburn and his men-at-arms."

"Aye, that was me," replied the giant. "I am glad to see you got away alive."

"And ever since I have been wishing we could meet again so I might thank you," said Robin. "Tell me your name."

"John of Melton," said the giant, but he spoke almost as if he were ashamed of the sound of it.

"And I am Robin Hood," said Robin, holding out his hand.

This time it was the giant who gasped. He eyed Robin from head to toe and gave a grim chuckle.

"Robin Hood," he repeated slowly. "That is a name I hear spoken with fear and trembling from Nottingham to Sherburn. And to think I nearly drowned you! I beg your pardon, great outlaw."

"And I will grant it, Little John," said Robin, "but only if tonight you eat supper with myself and my companions."

"Gladly," answered Little John, "for I no longer have a hearth of my own to go to."

"It sounds to me as if there is a tale in that," said Robin. "Perhaps you will tell it as we eat?"

2 The Giant's Tale

It was dark by the time Robin Hood and Little
John arrived in the clearing the outlaws called
the Camp of the Squirrels. The rest of the band
were there already, seated round a fire, and the
air was rich with a smell of simmering stew.

"So this is your home," remarked Little John.

"One of them," answered Robin. "We have
other camps over in Sherwood, for we never
like to stay long in one place."

As they walked towards the fire, Will
Scarlet sprang up to greet them.

"It is good to see you, Robin," he said. "None
of us are proud of the words that were spoken
this morning."

"This morning is forgotten," said Robin,

"and my wanderings have been rewarded, for I have here the man who saved my life in the market-place of Pontefract. Friends, I bid you make a place by the fire for Little John."

"No one could be more welcome," replied Will, "though I must say I cannot see what is little about him."

"Let us hope it is not his appetite," said Robin.

Yet Robin was right, for when supper was served, Little John showed no hunger. The outlaws plied him with a thick stew of venison and lentils, and with fresh barley buns from Swain the Baker's turf-covered oven, and with a mellow ale that had been rescued from a merchant who was taking it to market in Pontefract; but Little John sipped and pecked as if none of it tasted good to him.

"By my faith," exclaimed Robin, "you have a small stomach for a man so huge."

"Take no offence if I make a poor guest," answered Little John. "The truth is simply that I care no longer for the fruits of this earth."

"So I see," said Robin. "You said when we

19

met that you have no hearth to call your own. May I ask where you were bound when our paths crossed?"

"I was taking the first steps of a long journey," said Little John. "I am bound for the Holy Land."

"A noble quest," said Robin, "yet a pilgrim needs to eat if he is to reach his goal."

Little John stared into the fire. "It hardly matters if I get there or not," he replied. "All I ask is to live long enough to shake the dust of England off my feet."

"There is a story hidden in your words," said Robin, "and I guess it to be one of injustice and suffering. Many tales have been told around this fire, and if you wish to unlock your heart we will listen in silence."

Little John nodded thoughtfully, and ran his fingertips along a deep scar that marked the bald crown of his head. After a while he began to speak.

"It sometimes happens," he said, "that the happiness of those dear to him can mean more to a man than his own, and it goes by the same rule that their sorrows can break his heart. I was the shepherd of High Melton, and my master's daughter Clara was the apple of my eye. When she found love with a young knight named Adam, the sight of them together made my old heart creak with joy. They vowed to be married, but before it could come about, my master died and Clara was left an orphan."

Little John paused for a drink of ale.

"Now you all know the cruel law that says an heiress becomes the property of her overlord, and that is what happened to Clara. Earl William seized her and shut her up in his castle of Conisbrough. The law gives him the right to marry her to the man of his choice at the moment of his choice, and there the matter rests. Adam cannot help her, I cannot help her, and to tend my flocks within sight of the walls of Conisbrough is now more than I can bear."

"There is one thing in your tale that puzzles me," said Robin. "Amongst barons, Earl William has a name for being a just and honourable man."

"He may well be," said Little John, "but he spends most of the year on his lands in Sussex, leaving Conisbrough in the charge of a knight named Ernald of Mort. It is Ernald who seized Clara in the earl's name, and no one has ever mistaken Ernald for a just and honourable man."

Robin sat forward. "Then he deserves a poke in the eye," he said. "I say we go and free this maiden from her cage. Who comes with me?"

22

"Wait just a moment," begged Will Scarlet. "Have you ever seen the castle at Conisbrough? It has the highest walls and the tallest tower in the land."

"I am with you, Robin," said Much the Miller's son.

"And I," said Dickon; but the other outlaws, who were older and more wary, looked from Will to Robin, then back to Will, and Will gave a long, low groan.

"Oh Robin," he said. "You ask the earth."

"That I know," said Robin, "yet when we first became brothers of the forest we vowed to use our strength to help those in need, even at the risk of our lives. I will ask no man to come with me on a venture he thinks is folly, and I have never been one for rash boasts over a cup of ale. Much, go and saddle me one of our horses. Tonight I have some riding to do."

"Where are you going?" asked Will.

"Never you mind," said Robin, "and never fear. I will be back by daybreak. Little John, I trust you will spend the night here as our guest?"

Little John nodded in some bewilderment as Much emerged from the trees leading the brotherhood's finest mount, a grey stallion fit for a king. Robin pulled on his gloves, patted the horse's neck, and swung himself up into the saddle.

"Take every care," begged Will. "I do not like this business."

Robin reached down and clasped his friend by the hand. "Nor do I like to think of Ernald of Mort breaking a maiden's heart," he said.

And with that he rode off into the night.

3   A Glimpse of the Prison

The streets of the old town of Conisbrough were
dark and silent as Robin tethered his horse by
the church and made his way to where he could
look across at the hill on which stood Earl
William's castle.

What he saw made his stomach go cold, for
the arched gateway of the castle was flanked by
two round towers, and on either side were high
walls that ran from tower to tower in a ring
that encircled the hilltop. Rising above the
walls was the tallest keep-tower he had ever
seen. In the moonlight it had the look of a
smooth pillar of stone, and the chinks of light
that showed through the shuttered slits of its
windows seemed as far out of reach as the stars

in the night sky.

"So Will was right," said Robin to himself. "I can see now why Little John turned away in despair."

Behind him he heard a calling of farewells, and looking round he saw a burly man in a friar's robes swaying out of the doorway of a tavern. The friar walked over to a washing-trough, splashed his face heartily, then straightened and stretched and looked curiously at Robin.

"A blessing on you, good sir," said the friar. "Has something of note happened in the sky tonight, or do you make a habit of standing around gazing at the moon?"

"I was gazing at Earl William's castle," answered Robin. "There is a maiden within those walls I wish to meet."

The friar nodded gravely. "I have often wondered," he said, "why the wickedest of knights should have the fairest of the maidens — not, of course, that it is any real concern of a holy man like myself. I fear you would be well advised to forget this maiden of yours."

26

"Are the castle gates never open to strangers?" asked Robin.

"Only on Sundays," replied the friar. "The earl is so proud of his new chapel that he likes to fill it with worshippers, though even then I imagine you would need to be a richly-dressed knight to be allowed through its door."

"Well, I thank you for your advice," said Robin.

"You are most welcome," replied the friar.

"If you wish to repay me, remember me in your prayers. I need all the help I can get."

Robin rode out of Conisbrough by a road that led not to the forest, but to the village where he had been born. He was soon riding with lowered eyes past the fields that had been his in the days before he was outlawed, and he tethered his horse in the woods behind the house of Sir Gilbert Fitzwalter.

As he stepped into Sir Gilbert's orchard, he saw a huge wolfhound loping towards him with its ears pricked up in suspicion. Robin knelt down and beckoned to it.

"Come now, Sigurd you old monster," he called softly. "Surely you remember me?" The wolfhound leapt forward, and a moment later had its paws on Robin's shoulders and was licking his face.

"Now," said Robin, "let us see if we can find a way of letting Marian know I am here without waking the whole household."

It was not long after midsummer, and the apples on the trees were still young and green. Robin twisted one from its branch and threw

it so that it thumped against the shutters of
Marian's chamber, and as he did so he hooted
like an owl. To make an echo he threw a second
apple, with a second owl's call to keep it
company.

Before long the door of the house was edged
open, and Marian came running towards him
through the moonlight. Over her shift of white
linen she had pinned a mantle embroidered
with flowers, but Robin barely noticed, for his
eyes went to her face. His arms stretched out
towards her, and as he clasped her tight he was

the happiest man in all Christendom.

When they had spoken words of love, and poured out the longing for each other that they carried in their hearts, Robin told her of Little John and of the maiden imprisoned in the castle of Conisbrough.

"The answer is clear," said Marian: "To pass through the gates of Conisbrough you will have to become a knight."

Robin laughed and kissed her. "And where, my love," he asked, "am I to find a coat of chain mail and all the other finery that go to make a knight?"

"Perhaps," said Marian, "you could borrow them from a man who is now our most eager visitor, Sir Guy of Gisburn."

"Is this true?" asked Robin, looking around as if the house had become tainted. "Sir Guy comes here?"

"He thinks we are his friends," replied Marian. "Ever since the day we tricked him in Pontefract, he believes that my father and I have the same hatred for you in our hearts that he carries in his own. I am happy he should

31

think so, for whenever he is here with us I know that you are safe."

"Still, I do not see how that can help," said Robin.

"You and Sir Guy are of much the same build," said Marian. "If you were to shave off your beard, then crop your hair short the way he wears his, then ride up to Conisbrough wearing his chain-mail and colours . . ."

"My love," said Robin, "your wits are sharper than the east wind."

"Let me tell him that your mother has brought us a message that you wish to meet with him," suggested Marian. "Where shall I say you wish the meeting to be?"

Robin thought for a moment, then broke into a smile.

"At Wentbridge," he answered, "on the highroad, where there is a grange of white monks. There could be no better place."

4 Trickery at Wentbridge

So it came about that on the following Sunday, Sir Guy of Gisburn left Pontefract before daybreak, riding at the head of a dozen men-at-arms too sleepy to grumble at the way they had been ordered from their beds.

Riding beside Sir Guy was his sergeant-at-arms, a grim old warrior by the name of Serlo.

"Where are we bound?" he asked Sir Guy.

"To Wentbridge," replied the knight. "The outlaw Robin Hood has sent word that he wishes to meet with me."

"It has the smell of a trap," said Serlo.

"Indeed," agreed Sir Guy, "which is why I wish to get there early, and set a trap of my own."

"What do you have in mind?" asked the sergeant.

"Something sweet and simple," said Sir Guy. "I want you and the men to hide in the woods with your crossbows at the ready, and when Robin Hood shows himself, I want you to shoot him as full of arrows as if he were Saint Sebastian."

"That sounds simple enough," agreed Serlo. "Leave it to us."

In the damp summer dawn they reached the rim of a wooded valley, and found themselves looking down on the village of Wentbridge. At a nod from Sir Guy, Serlo led the men-at-arms off the road into the trees, and the knight rode on down the hill alone.

When he reached the bridge he dismounted, and turning his horse loose to graze in the meadows, he leaned against the parapet and let his eyes rove over the village. He knew the place well. To one side of the road lay the walled grange with its chapel and cluster of farm buildings, while on the other stood an inn and a few ramshackle houses. Despite the monks, Wentbridge had an evil name, and travellers never stopped there after dark; but in the gathering sunlight, with his men-at-arms hidden in the woods at his back, Sir Guy felt as bold as a lion.

Almost at once he saw a man emerge from the gateway of the grange and come walking towards him. He wore a forester's tunic of Lincoln green, but his face was clean-shaven and his hair cropped short, and in no way did he look like a man of the woods. It was by the sword hanging from his belt, a sword the knight had once seen drawn against him, that Sir Guy knew his man.

"Well met, Robin Hood," he said calmly.

"Well met, Sir Guy," replied Robin, coming to a halt twenty paces away, at the far end of the bridge.

"You make a fine target," said Sir Guy with a smile.

"So do you," answered Robin.

The smile withered on Sir Guy's lips as a second man dressed in green stepped out from under the trailing branches of a willow tree by the water's edge. He carried a longbow, with an an arrow notched to the string, and as he

walked forward he raised the bow so that the arrow pointed straight at Sir Guy's throat.

"You may remember my friend, Will Scarlet," said Robin. "Take my word for it that he never misses his mark."

Sir Guy waited until the outlaws were standing side by side at the far end of the bridge, then he threw himself to the ground.

"Shoot them both!" he yelled.

But nothing happened. No crossbow bolts hissed through the air to break the calm of the summer morning, and before Sir Guy could save himself, Robin had leapt on top of him and drawn the knight's sword from his scabbard. A moment later Sir Guy was being tickled under the chin by the tip of his own sword-blade.

"Now Sir Guy," said Robin, "you may rise very slowly to your feet. One rash move and your head goes flying into the river."

The knight could do nothing but obey, and as he stood up he shuddered with the same cold fear that he had spent his life inflicting on others. Looking round he saw his men-at-arms, stripped of their weapons, being chased out of the woods by a band of monks. At first he could hardly believe his eyes, but when he blinked and looked again he saw that the monks were bearded and carried longbows. One of them was so huge that his monk's habit barely came down to his knees.

"What devilry is this?" asked Sir Guy.

"I would call it a miracle," said Robin Hood. "We asked the monks for the loan of their clothes, then locked them into their chapel. When we left them they were saying their prayers as if nothing had happened."

The men-at-arms were herded onto the bridge, and Sir Guy came face to face with Serlo, who smiled sourly.

"Have you anything to say for yourself?" Sir Guy asked him.

"Not a lot," answered Serlo. "One moment we heard monks walking down the road singing a psalm, and the next we were surrounded by wild men with longbows."

"Get these pigs into the grange," shouted Robin. "Much and Dickon, run back up the hill and get their horses."

Once inside the grange, Sir Guy and his men were prodded and poked into a corner of the courtyard. The outlaws shaped themselves into a line, and their arrows were still notched to their bows.

"Now," said Robin, "I want you to strip to

your shirts, and to throw your clothes and armour into a heap."

"You can burn in hell first," retorted Sir Guy.

"I fear you would get there before me," said Robin, "but I have no time to argue. We can always take the clothes from your dead bodies, if that is how you wish it to be."

The outlaws raised their bows and took aim.

"What do we do?" Serlo asked his master.

Sir Guy looked thoughtfully at the outlaws, and the one who impressed him most was as tall as a giant and grinning from ear to ear, as if he could hardly wait to loose his arrow.

"We do whatever they want," muttered Sir Guy.

Helmets and belts, metal-ringed hauberks and boots and hose: all were pulled off and thrown into a heap, until Sir Guy and his men stood barefoot in their shirts. The outlaws roared with laughter, and Robin unbolted the heavy door of one of the farm buildings and swung it open.

"We can hardly let you wander the roads

41

unarmed," said Robin. "You would be quite at the mercy of the wicked robbers who live in the forest. So for your own protection we will shut you up in here with the other swine."

Before Sir Guy could protest he was flung into a dark and stinking barn. His men were pushed in on top of him, and as the door was slammed and bolted, they slithered around and fell over each other. Hogs bit their ankles in the blackness, and as soon as he found his way back to what felt like the door, Sir Guy hammered on it with his fists.

"I swear you will pay for this," he shouted. "Do you hear me, Robin Hood? Do you hear me?"

But there was no reply.

5   The Dark Tower

As the bells summoning the faithful to Mass
rang out over the castle and town of
Conisbrough, a group of horsemen drew rein on
the edge of the town. Anyone who saw them
from afar would have taken them for Sir Guy
of Gisburn and his men-at-arms.

Sweating inside Sir Guy's helmet like a mop
in a bucket, Robin turned to his companions.

"This is as far as we ride together," he told
them. "Little John will come with me into the
castle. The rest of you must wait in the town.
If I blow on my horn, make for the gateway,
for it means we are in trouble, and if we get out
in one piece we will need you there to shoot
down whoever is hard on our heels."

43

Will Scarlet rolled his eyes to heaven. "May luck go with you," he said miserably.

Robin Hood and Little John rode on through the town and took the track that climbed towards the castle gateway.

"It is strange how the walls look higher in daylight," said Robin.

"I may not even reach them," muttered Little John. "This coat of chain mail is killing me."

"We are almost there," said Robin. "Try to look proud and magnificent."

The hooves of their horses clattered onto the timbers of the drawbridge.

"Make way for Sir Guy of Gisburn!" cried Little John, and the guards in the shadows of the gateway took one look at their finery and stood back to let them pass.

As they entered the castle-yard they saw it was crowded with horses and wagons and servants rushing to and fro. Robin beckoned with a knightly gloved hand to a boy who was on his way to the kitchens with a rack of hares.

"Tell me," he said haughtily, "why are there so many people here today?"

"Earl William returned last night," answered the boy as he hurried past.

"Saints preserve us," said Little John. "He never travels with less than eighty men-at-arms."

"That could be a blessing in disguise," said Robin. "Ernald of Mort may hardly notice two more strangers. We have timed it well. It seems they are all in the chapel." As they dismounted he gazed around the halls that stood against the battlements. "Where do we look for your maiden?" he asked. "She could be in any one of a hundred chambers."

"Meg says that Ernald keeps her shut up in the keep," said Little John.

Robin spun round. "Who is Meg?" he asked, but Little John was already striding across the castle-yard towards the thick, high tower that looked a fortress in itself.

The doorway of the tower was high above the ground, and they climbed to it by a narrow stair of stone. Little John twisted the iron ring

of the door handle and gave a snarl of dismay.

"Locked," he said.

"Locked from outside," said Robin, "which means that it is closed by a single bolt. If we could only break the bolt . . ."

"With God's help it will be done," said Little John.

They waited until a sound of chanting came from the chapel, then Little John stood back and began to breathe fast and deep. His nostrils flared, his fists clenched, and the veins stood out on his wrists. At the seventh breath he stepped forward, kicking high with his right leg, and brought his foot slamming down on the lock. The oaken door shuddered, and with a splintering of wood it swung open, while the lock, smashed from its frame, dropped with a clink into the yard.

"This is truly a day of miracles," said Robin.

They found themselves in a dark and empty chamber, and turned at once to follow a stair-passage that twisted up through the thick stone walls. Narrow shafts of light came slanting in through the windows, but there were so few windows that it seemed as if they were climbing into a tomb. The passage led them to a second chamber, where again there was no one to be seen, and they hurried on up the stairs into the chamber above.

There, as they entered, they heard prayers being spoken by two soft voices. Set into the walls of the tower was a small vaulted chapel, and kneeling by the altar were a woman in simple clothes and a maiden with long braided hair and a face as pale as snow. Little John tore the helmet from his head.

"Have no fear, Meg," he said. "It is only me."

"John," exclaimed the woman, clapping her hands to her face. Robin turned to meet the widening blue eyes of the maiden.

"You must be the lady Clara," he said with a smile. "John did not tell me of your beauty."

"This is my good friend Robin Hood," said Little John. "We have come to take you away from here."

"Is this true?" asked Clara.

"It may be," said Robin, "if we hurry."

He led them quickly down through the tower

and out into the sunlight of the castle-yard. As they walked towards the horses, the doors of the chapel were thrown open, and out spilled a crowd of over a hundred knights and ladies and men-at-arms.

"Too late," said Little John. "We are trapped."

49

"Not yet," said Robin, and he spoke under his breath to Meg and Clara. "Keep walking towards the horses . . ."

"Who goes there?" cried a voice from the crowd, and its owner was a knight with a swarthy face who came striding towards them.

"I am Guy of Gisburn," cried Robin, "and I challenge you to combat, Ernald of Mort, in the name of the maiden you have so cruelly imprisoned."

A second knight, who Robin guessed to be Earl William, came hurrying forward. "What is the meaning of this?" he demanded. "No maiden has ever been wronged in my castle."

"Sir Ernald has betrayed your trust, my lord earl," said Robin.

Sir Ernald's eyes narrowed into slits in a mask of anger. "Men to arms!" he yelled. "Seize the intruders! Bar the gate!"

Yet even as he spoke, the air hissed and it was as if the sky filled with serpents of smoke. Over their heads flew ten burning arrows, to thud one after another into the roof of the chapel. Around their shafts were tied rags

soaked in pitch, which splashed over the roof-
timbers like golden rain. Robin looked up to see
Will Scarlet and nine of the outlaws standing
on a tower high above the gateway, loosing a
second volley of arrows towards a hall on the
other side of the yard. The air filled with smoke.

"Fire!" screamed Earl William. "Fetch water!
Save my chapel!"

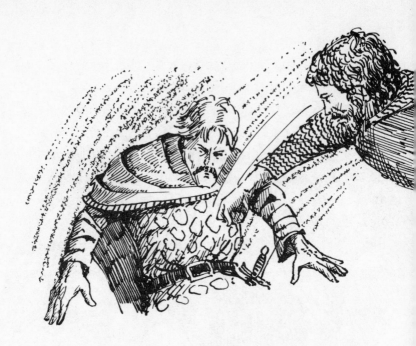

Men ran in all directions, and only Ernald of
Mort stood his ground. He looked from the
chapel roof to the archers on the battlements,
then at Robin, and made to draw his sword.
Before his hand could clasp the hilt he caught a
blow from a giant fist that knocked him
straight out of the daylight into night.

Little John rubbed his knuckles and turned
to Robin. "Shall we take our leave?" he asked.

"It would certainly be wrong to overstay our
welcome," agreed Robin.

Meg and Clara were ready with the horses, and a moment later the four of them were riding through the gateway where the guards had been tied up like turkeys. Will and the outlaws came running down the stairway from the tower and followed them out, and on the far side of the drawbridge they met Much and Dickon puffing up the hill dragging a wagon filled with kindling, which in no time at all had been pushed into the gateway and set alight.

"That should keep the wasps in their nest for a while," said Will Scarlet. "Well done, lads."

"What were you doing up on the battlements?" Robin asked him. "I thought I told you to wait in the town?"

Will scratched his chin. "Perhaps you did," he said. "My memory is not what it used to be."

"I hope you remember where you left your horses," said Robin.

And anyone who saw them from afar would have thought that Sir Guy of Gisburn and his men-at-arms were leaving Conisbrough in something of a hurry.

6   Hearts of the Forest

But Sir Guy of Gisburn and his men-at-arms
were still locked in the pigsty of the monks of
Wentbridge, and they were not in good cheer.
Hours had gone by, and they were beginning to
learn what it was like to be shut away in a
dungeon and forgotten.

"If ever we escape from here," said one of
them, "I vow never again to push men into
prison."

"And I vow to give all I have stolen back to
the poor," said another.

"Quiet, you fools," ordered Sir Guy.
"Something is happening outside."

In the courtyard they heard a milling of
horses, and the sound of voices raised in

laughter. Sir Guy hammered on the door with his fists, but no one paid him any heed, and they were still locked in darkness when silence returned to the grange.

Another long hour had passed when finally

the door was unbolted and opened by a white-haired monk who gasped at the sight of the prisoners.

"By Saint Bridget!" he cried. "A miracle! Our hogs are turning human!"

Sir Guy pushed past him and staggered out into the sunlight, followed by his muck-spattered men. Heaped in the centre of the yard they saw their clothes and armour.

"Where are our horses?" Sir Guy asked the monk.

"Horses? Ah, horses," murmured the monk, who was Brother Hubert. "I seem to remember seeing some horses grazing in the meadows by the river."

As soon as they had rummaged their way back into their clothes, Sir Guy led his men in search of their mounts. They were gathering them together when a cavalcade of knights came thundering down the road and galloped into the meadow to surround them.

"Throw down your weapons, Guy of Gisburn," ordered a knight, "and tell us where you have hidden the lady Clara."

"The lady Clara?" repeated Sir Guy. "I know no one of that name."

"We are in no mood to play games," replied the knight, and he signalled to his followers. "Tie them to their horses," he ordered. "They will speak soon enough under torture."

Nothing the men from Pontefract could say made any difference. They were dragged to the castle of Conisbrough and thrown at the feet of Earl William and Ernald of Mort.

"Have mercy, my lords," begged Sir Guy. "This is all a mistake."

"Are you not Guy of Gisburn?" asked Earl William.

"Yes," answered Sir Guy, "but I am not the man you seek."

Earl William sniffed at his prisoner. "It is true you do not smell like a knight," he admitted. "What do you have to say for yourself?"

So Sir Guy saved himself from torture, but only by telling the story of how he had been tricked out of his clothes by the outlaw Robin Hood. It was a story that travelled fast, and for a long time afterwards Sir Guy could go nowhere without hearing the sound of muffled laughter behind his back.

While all this was happening, Robin Hood and his companions came safely to their lair in the depths of the forest of Barnsdale. Waiting for them there were Marian and the young knight Adam, whom she had sought out in Melton, and found brooding over the maiden he thought he had lost forever.

At the sight of her true love, Clara gave a cry of delight, and jumped from her horse into his arms. Nor was Robin any slower in running to Marian.

"My love," said Robin, "your beauty lights up the forest. Will the day never come that you join us here?"

"The day will surely come," said Marian, "when I can stay away no longer; but in the meantime, you must come more often to pick the apples in my orchard."

They turned to see Clara and Adam standing before them.

"How can I thank you, Robin Hood?" asked Clara.

"Why only me?" asked Robin. "Thank John for leading me to you. Thank Marian for finding the ruse to get us through the gates. Thank Will and the brotherhood for saving our lives."

"I thank you all," cried Clara. "If there is any way I can help you, you have only to say."

"You can help us by finding safety," replied

Robin. "Do either of you have family who live beyond the reach of Ernald of Mort?"

"My father has lands in Cumbria," said Adam. "He will give us shield and shelter."

"Then you must travel there by lonely roads," said Robin. "Will Meg go with you?"

"She is my much loved nurse," answered Clara. "I would not dream of leaving her behind."

Out of the corner of his eye, Robin had seen Meg take Little John by the hand.

"You are a good man, John," said Meg. "Will you come with us?"

"Oh, my road lies elsewhere," said Little John, and Robin could see that it tore his heart to say it.

"We must be leaving," said Marian to the young ones. "I will set you on your road."

Meg nodded sadly, then stretched up on tiptoe to give Little John a kiss, and the giant turned as red as a berry.

When the farewells had been spoken, the outlaws watched their friends ride away through the forest. Little John stood like a man

unsure what to do next, and Robin reached up
and set his hand on the giant's shoulder.

"Little John," he said, "from all I have seen
I would say your heart is in the right place."

"So is yours," answered the giant.

"Then will you sup with us," asked Robin,
"before you take your road to the Holy Land?"

Little John folded his arms and glowered.
"Are you suggesting," he asked, "that I should
go flying off like a swan when there is plainly
some hard work to be done around here?"

"Never," said Robin, and he held out his
hand. Little John grinned and clasped it in a

giant's grip that made Robin yell with pain.

"By my faith," cried Robin. "You could crush a stone. I may never be able to draw my bow again."

But he did, and often, and Little John was always there to follow it with an arrow of his own. All the outlaws of the brotherhood felt stronger with a giant in their midst, but out of all the bonds of love and trust that were forged by their adventures, no two friends grew closer than did Robin Hood and Little John.